The Journey Inward

The Journey Inward
KEY TO EVERLASTING PEACE AND HAPPINESS

Charanjit Singh Sidhu

Amrit Press International

Amrit Press International
76835 Manor Lane
Palm Desert, California 92211-7123

Printed in the United States of America

ISBN:0-615-47552-3
ISBN-13:978-0-615-47552-3

DEDICATION

Thanks to everyone who made this book possible—my family, particularly my wife, Meet, for allowing me to pursue my passion, and my two wonderful kids, Sanjog and Eknoor, who provide such great opportunities to be patient, joyful, and loving.

Most of all this book is dedicated to you, the reader, who is searching for a "better way." Those who ask will always receive!

Love to all,

Charanjit Singh

CONTENTS

PREFACE

The story *The Journey Inward: Key to Everlasting Peace and Happiness* is written in the form of a spiritual fiction. Although the characters are make-believe, the teachings introduced in the story come from a real-life spiritual path. The characters in the story serve as examples of how the practice of this spiritual path can lead to great transformation in one's life.

My hope is for you to be both entertained and moved by this experience, and perhaps, to be inspired enough to embrace one of the most powerful teachings in the world.

Charanjit S. Sidhu

CHAPTER ONE
THE FLASH FORWARD

George quietly walks into the room where he sees his mother's frail body, with tubes running through it, laying motionless on the bed. He walks up to her and grabs one of her hands, placing it in his. His mother's eyes open gently, and her gaze falls immediately on George. As they both look at each other, tears fill their eyes. *How could this happen?* George thinks to himself. *How could this be happening to the only one bright spot in my life? Life can't be this unfair. Where's the hope? Where's the compassion in all this? Where the heck is God!*

CHAPTER TWO
A LIFE OF PAIN

For George Harris life was a struggle with no way out. He secretly wished for a better way. George grew up in Bronx County, New York. He came from a middle-class family who hardly spent much time together because George's father was a traveling salesman. And when George did spend time with his father, it usually involved being chewed out for not doing well in school. George was a terrible student, and a loner. Bullies constantly teased him. Through his difficulties he had one thing he could rely on, and that was his mother. She was a warm and gentle person, who comforted George throughout his struggles. She would remind him that it did not matter how well he did in school as long as he made an honest effort to do his very best. However, to his father and the outside world, his very best was never enough.

George's trouble in making friends and passing classes persisted in high school. At Christopher Columbus High School, he made a few friends, but was hardly noticed by the main group of students in his class. George had a very reserved nature and found it difficult to open up to people around him. He avoided school-related social events, for the thought of being around a large group of people frightened George. In class George was a daydreamer and would constantly watch the clock. He could not wait to get home to read his comic books. For George, the books served as an escape from everyday life.

George barely graduated from high school and managed to get into a state university, mainly due to his family's poor financial condition. He attended Empire State College, where he spent more time trying to make friends than he did studying. Therefore he constantly fell behind in his studies. However, due to his persistent nature, he always found a way to pass his classes and completed a four-year degree in business.

After college it was time for George to find a job. George's father knew that his failure of a son would not be able to find a job on his own. So he took the initiative and found George an outside sales position with A-1 Building Products, a small family-operated business specializing in commercial and residential building materials. The owner of the company knew George's father from the days when they were both salesmen. Since the company was located in New York City, George could continue to live at home.

It is the weekend before George's first day on the job. George is extremely nervous and unable to eat or sleep. On Sunday George wakes up early and heads to the bathroom to brush his teeth. He stands over the sink and pauses to look at himself in the mirror.

He sees a young man, overweight with pale white skin and dark curly hair. George, now twenty-three years of age, hardly looks old enough to go out and work in the real world.

Later George is downstairs in the kitchen having a cup of coffee when his mother walks in. She sees George sitting quietly at the table and staring out into space. "You're up early George!"

"I was thinking about tomorrow and what it will be like on my first day at the job."

"Are you worried, George?" his mother asks, putting on her apron.

"Actually Mom, I'm not sure if this job is right for me. Dad suggested I go into sales, but what do I know about selling and building clients? I'd rather work at a job that I can enjoy and in which I'll make a difference."

George's mother looks gently at George and says, "Well George, I don't think you have to worry about whether you're going to make a difference or not. I have raised you to be a sensitive and caring person. I'm very proud of the way you have turned out. In the end it's not important what job you do, but how you do it." George sips his coffee listening carefully to his mother.

"You see, George, every job involves interacting with people, whether you're a teacher, accountant, or janitor. The difference you make is by how you treat others while you go about your daily routine. And I know you will be patient, kind, and respectful with all the people you meet."

George, feeling reassured, stands up and gives his mother a big, warm hug. He can't imagine what his life would be without his mother. Suddenly George's father walks in and sees the two embracing.

"So George, you ready for your big day tomorrow?" his father asks, making his way to the kitchen table.

"Yes, I am, Dad."

"Good!" his father responds as he puts his hand firmly on George's back. "Now promise you will make me proud. I have gone out of my way to land you this job. So don't let me down!"

"Alright, Dad," responds George, as he starts to feel the nervousness creep back into the pit of his stomach.

CHAPTER THREE
THE GOOD LIFE

Doug Peterson was born into a traditional American family. He grew up in a suburban mansion in Westchester County, New York, with a white picket fence and dog. His father was a successful lawyer at a firm located in downtown New York. His mother, a typical homemaker, was beautiful, and she loved to take care of the needs of her family. Doug was the youngest child. He had two older siblings, Mary, the middle child, and Josh, the older brother. It was not uncommon to see friends and family dropping by to visit the Petersons. For Doug life could not have given him a better scenario for enjoying the fruits of the "American Dream."

As time passed all three Peterson children attended prestigious private schools, the kind of places that bred the future leaders of the country. Not only was Doug Peterson adored at school because of the popularity of his older siblings, but Doug himself possessed a charming personality from early in life. He found it very easy to make friends and catch the eye of girls at school. His popularity and ability to make friends followed him through high school. He attended the prestigious Masters School, where he was the school president as well as the president of the math club. And because of his charm and good looks, he dated Victoria Harper, the blonde cheerleading idol of every boy in school.

After high school Doug attended Princeton University. With the freedom to spend time as he wished, Doug enjoyed college life to its fullest. He spent his time in sports bars and house parties with his fraternity brothers and still managed to pass his classes with C's. Middling grades at Princeton were more than enough to land him a job with Wright & Co., a New York City investment firm right on Wall Street. In his first couple of years, he spent his time working hard, impressing his clients and superiors, and making a six-figure income. He also spent time partying hard with socialites, meeting various beautiful women, and vacationing at remote places around the world.

Doug, now twenty-four years of age is the epitome of the All-American young man. He stands over six feet tall and has sandy brown hair, blue eyes, and a chiseled face.

Doug is invited for a weekend to the Bahamas by Dale Whitmore, a senior partner of Wright & Co. Dale is a single middle-aged man who is always accompanied on his excursions by a group of attractive young woman. Doug is invited not only to enjoy a good time, but to use his talents to cement relationships with business clients who will be present at the gatherings.

Nightly everyone meets at Mr. Whitmore's private bungalow for socializing. The bungalow has a festive mood as everyone comes dressed in bright colors. The private bar is well-stocked with spirits and wine.

On one particular evening, Doug enters the party exotically dressed in a Hawaiian shirt, white linen slacks, and leather sandals. He wastes no time in exhibiting his charm. Doug mingles first with the key players of his firm's clients. He woos them over with his knowledge of new investment strategies promising higher returns on the dollar. "Listen gentlemen, if you want to remain stuck in the status quo, then keep doing what you're comfortable doing. But if you're brave enough, then take my hand and I will lead you to that path of unlimited potential and growth." The executives are mesmerized by Doug's charm and hopes of a brighter future.

Next Doug moves over to the bar and mixes his favorite drink, gin and tonic. He then walks up to a group of young ladies standing in the room almost waiting for Doug to seduce them. Doug wastes no opportunity to go in for the kill. He focuses his gaze on the women and says, "I must say the beauty of the islands can't compare with the beauty I see in front of me." The women respond with school-girl giggles.

As the night winds down, Doug narrows the women down to one. He pulls her to the side and tries to soften her up with his smooth talk. "You don't look like the type of girl I'd expect at these gatherings."

"I was invited by my cousin, who is a regular at these parties," the woman explains, pulling her hair back from her face. "I am not like

9

the other girls here. I don't go around sleeping with every guy who sweeps me off my feet."

Doug butts in and says, "Look, I am here to have a good time, and I'm not interested in engaging in a moral discussion. So if you don't mind, I need to fill up my drink." Doug leaves the young woman standing alone, looking dazed and confused. He moves over to another woman standing near the bar. "So what's a lovely young lady like you doing standing here all alone?" The woman responds with a big smile. Later Doug can be seen leaving the bungalow with the young lady wrapped tightly around his arm, and no doubt he is on his way to another conquest.

CHAPTER FOUR

THERE MUST BE A BETTER WAY!

One day as Doug is out for an early morning jog, he sees an innocent but powerful scene unfold in front of him. He sees a man coming out of a beat-up truck wearing a custodial uniform. The man then opens the passenger door to let out what appears to be his young daughter. It seems they're spending some free time together before they both go on to their daily routine. The man picks up the girl from inside the truck with great joy and takes her to the community park. Both are thrilled as they make their way to the playground. The two enjoy great fun together and are totally oblivious to the outside world.

As Doug jogs he finds himself hypnotized by this scene and not able to take his eyes off the father and daughter. He is surprised how a simple gathering between two persons could be so joyful. As he continues to jog, he mentally reviews his life. *Is my life really making me happy?* Doug thinks to himself. *I feel like I have everything I want, but deep down inside I feel this emptiness that I can't explain.* He wonders, *If my life continues in the same direction, will this strange feeling of lack ever disappear?*

Later at work Doug approaches the office of Stewart Wright, the lead partner of Wright & Co. Doug asks if he can come in. As Doug sits down, Mr. Wright starts to commend him for his work and tells him what an asset he is to the firm. Then he asks Doug how he can help him. Doug asks Mr. Wright what he sees for him in the future. Mr. Wright responds by saying, "Doug, I see a lot of myself in you. You are a lot like me when I was your age. You're a hard worker, and you know how to impress your clients, so if you continue working hard there's no reason why you won't be sitting in my seat one day."

Mr. Wright sees a concerned look on Doug's face and asks if he had another question on his mind. Doug responds by saying, "Sir, are you happy?"

"What do you mean, 'Am I happy?'" says Mr. Wright.

"Sir, I want to know if you are truly happy in life."

Mr. Wright pauses and then looks at Doug and says, "I'm happy to be a partner in this firm, to be married to a beautiful wife, and be the honorary president of the local country club. Sure! I'm happy."

"Sir, please don't get me wrong," Doug explains, learning forward in his chair. "But what if all the things you're happy about were taken from you. Would you still be happy?"

Mr. Wright thinks about it for a moment and says, "Don't be ridiculous! It took years of hard work to attain all this, and therefore it can't be taken away so easily."

Doug did not press any further but felt his question had not been answered. As he walked out of the office, he saw his future turning out to be exactly like Mr. Wright's—great job, beautiful wife, honorary president of some golf club, and sitting in front of a large desk not really knowing if he was happy or not.

CHAPTER FIVE

THE ANSWER!

As for George Harris, life marches on as a meaningless journey with no ray of hope. Although he takes a positive attitude to work everyday, he is greatly affected by the pressures of his new job. Pete Wilson, George's boss, is very demanding and short-tempered. He never skips an opportunity to criticize George for his work. He constantly tells George, "Son, to be successful in sales you have to have a killer attitude. Being nice will get you nowhere in this business. You have to hound your clients until you get them to say yes."

In addition to Mr. Wilson's criticism, George is easily upset by the rejections he receives from his potential clients. After each rejection George doubts whether he has the heart to carry on with this job. He can't see himself becoming more aggressive and pushy with his prospective clients. *I can't just change my personality for the worse*, George thinks to himself. *What do I need to do! How can I cope with these pressures at work? How can I make it all happen without losing my mind?*

One night after a long day of work, George decides to get a bite to eat at a downtown sports bar. Television screens hung high on the walls are showing the Yankees' game. George notices another young man in a shirt and tie sitting a couple of bar stools away. Both men sip on their beer while they glance at a beautiful waitress serving drinks nearby. The young man looks at George and says, "So what do you think? Is she your type?"

George answers, "She's female. That's good enough for me!" Both enjoy a laugh together. The young man walks up to a stool near George and asks him if he can buy him another beer. He then sticks out his hand and confidently introduces himself as Doug Peterson. The two sit together and enjoy their beers. They talk about work and where they grew up. As they pound back more beer, they start to open up and talk about deeper stuff. George tells Doug how his life up until now has been nothing but a struggle, and how he wishes things could take a turn for the better. Doug tells George that having things go your way does not necessarily convert into happiness. "Look at me," he tells George. "I went to Princeton, and I landed a six-figure salaried job at an investment firm. I have always been popular, always had girlfriends. Shouldn't I be happy? But it feels empty. I've been asking myself if there isn't more to all this, to life. These things won't last, and they haven't made me happy. There must be a way or answer out there that leads us to lasting peace and happiness."

"Well, if you can find the answer, I'll be more than glad to hear it," George responds, pulling back the last of his beer.

The Answer!

Doug tells George it was a pleasure talking to him and gives him his business card. "If you ever need help in making investment decisions, please don't hesitate to call." As George sits and looks at the business card, he gets a strange feeling that he will meet this man again.

A few days later, George is walking down the street after meeting a business client. He notices a flyer posted on the window of a bookstore. The flyer gives information about an author book signing. The title of the books is *Change Your Life from the Inside Out.* George walks into the bookstore and finds a copy of the book in the New Age section. He takes time to read some of the chapter headings: "Happiness is a Choice, You're Not a Victim, Teach Only Love," and "Peace Starts with You." Although George is somehow drawn to the words, he is a little embarrassed and puts the book back on the shelf before someone notices him. As he walks out, he grabs a copy of the flyer. The same night George calls up Doug and invites him to the book signing.

Doug and George meet at the bookstore. They wait in line to meet the guest author. The two seem somewhat out of place because most of the people in line are either senior citizens or women. As the two get closer to the front of the line, they catch a peek of a woman sitting behind a desk signing books and talking to fans. She is a middle-aged woman with short, curly brown hair. Finally it is Doug and George's turn to meet the author. The woman welcomes them with a warm smile and introduces herself as Helen Davies. She tells them she is delighted to see them at her book signing.

George speaks first and tells Helen that they are both looking to find a better way. Helen tells them that most people want to find a purpose to life. She says, "Without a meaningful purpose, life can seem like a struggle with no way out." She tells the two young men that the material in her book has helped her and many others to find a purpose and bring more peace and happiness into their lives. Helen notices that two young men do not have a book to sign. So she invites them to a workshop she is presenting in town.

Doug and George decide to attend the workshop, which is held at a local community center. There are about twenty to thirty people in attendance. They wait eagerly to hear this well-known, local author. Helen approaches the microphone to greet the audience but realizes the microphone is too high up. Some chuckles arise from the audience as they realize how short Helen is. Finally Helen is able to adjust the microphone to a proper height. She starts by saying, "I'm sorry everyone, it runs in the family."

She then introduces herself and tells a little about herself and how her book came about. She tells the audience the material from her book is inspired by a great spiritual text, which she will introduce them to a little later. Helen tells the audience that she hopes that her book will inspire them to read this spiritual classic. She then pauses and says, "The reason you are all here is because you have chosen at some level to make a change in your life. We all seek a sense of purpose, meaningful relationships, and peace and happiness in our lives. Although we have searched for these things, we have not found them in any lasting way. Relationships have fallen, money and jobs have been lost, and other problems constantly fill our daily lives. So how are we ever to have peace in our lives if such things seem so fleeting?"

The audience, completely still, listens carefully as Helen continues to speak. "I believe we have been programmed by the world to look for happiness outside of us. But since the world is always changing, we can never rely on the world to bring us this goal. Instead I believe we have to shift our focus and journey inward to find the happiness that we deserve. You see, peace and happiness cannot be found by changing our outer world; instead it can be found by changing the way we look at the world." Helen pauses to pull a thick blue book from the under the podium. "I would like to read from a book that has tremendously changed my life and that was the inspiration for my new book. This book I am holding here is titled *A Course in Miracles*. You may be asking what a miracle is. A miracle is simply changing from a fearful to a loving perception of the world. This simple change can lead to a dramatic experience in which you are no longer the victim of the world you see. In fact, a passage in *A Course in Miracles* reads, 'I am not a victim of the world I see.' The *Course* emphasizes forgiving others and ourselves as the path to peace. But this is not the traditional type of forgiveness in which you forgive people for what they have done to you. Instead it has to do with how you look at others and the world around you."

Next Helen opens to a page in the book and reads, "What could you want that forgiveness cannot give? Do you want peace? Forgiveness offers it. Do you want happiness, a quiet mind, a certainty of purpose, and a sense of worth and beauty that transcends the world? Do you want care and safety and the warmth of sure protection always? Do you want a quietness that cannot be disturbed, a gentleness that never can be hurt, a deep, abiding comfort, and a rest so perfect it can never be upset? All this, forgiveness offers you."

Helen continues, "The *Course* is a self-study course that helps the student systematically train his mind to choose peace instead of conflict. And through study and application of the *Course*, the student realizes everything he sees is the result of his thoughts. Therefore the cause of the world is seen in the student's mind and not outside. Once the cause is identified, the student can do something to change his thinking and inevitably the world he sees."

Helen pauses for a moment and says, "To put it simply, ladies and gentlemen, change your thinking and you will see a different world. This shift in emphasis from what we perceive outside to what we see inside is the key to finding lasting peace and happiness."

For the remainder of the workshop, Helen gives practical examples for applying the teachings of the *Course* on a daily basis. Doug and George are fascinated by the information given at the workshop. They both are convinced that this is the answer that they have been searching for.

CHAPTER SIX
INDECENT PROPOSAL

A few days later, Doug is invited to attend a party hosted by a prospective business client of the firm. Along with the partners, a few of the other top-notch performers of the firm are invited to attend the gathering. The party is hosted at the home of Mr. and Mrs. Charles Wilmington. Mr. Wilmington is the founder and now board member of Wilmington Global Enterprises Inc., a successful import export company in town.

Doug enters the party well dressed in a business suit and is greeted by the Wilmington's butler. He spots some of his colleagues and partners from his firm, walks up to them, and shakes their hands. Then one of the partners takes Doug and introduces him to Mr. and Mrs. Wilmington. Later on Doug is enjoying himself and sipping on a drink when he sees Mrs. Wilmington glancing at him from a distance. Mrs. Wilmington is an elegant and attractive woman who is much younger than her husband. As Doug is standing alone and enjoying his drink, Mrs. Wilmington walks up to him. "So Doug, are you enjoying yourself?"

"Yes I am, Mrs. Wilmington."

"Oh Doug, enough of that Mrs. Wilmington stuff. Please call me Sharon."

Doug, now feeling more comfortable, tells Sharon what a lovely home she has.

"Well, thank you, Doug. Would you like to see more of the place?"

Doug, being polite, tells her he would love to. Next Sharon walks him out to the back terrace, where they enjoy the view of the Wilmington estate. As the two are enjoying a light conversation, Sharon looks at Doug and says, "How about I give you a little tour of our private guesthouse? There is a cute little bar set up inside you might enjoy."

Doug, now uncomfortable, says, "Thank you, but I'd rather keep enjoying the view from the terrace."

"Now come on Doug, I saw you looking at me across the room."

"I'm sorry, Sharon, but I meant nothing by it."

Next Sharon places both her hands on Doug's chest and says, "Look dear, spending some private time with me will be great for your career."

"I am sorry, but I can't do that," replies Doug.

As Doug starts to makes his way back to the party, Sharon grabs Doug's hand and tells him that she always gets what she wants.

Doug quietly walks back inside. He gathers himself and then tells one of his senior partners that he needs to leave early. The partner replies, "Doug, you party pooper, why go home so early?" Then he looks at Doug's face and says, "Alright, you look a little pale, so go home and get some rest."

Later that night Sharon tells her husband that a young man from the investment firm offered to sleep with her in exchange for business with his company. When she refused he immediately left the party upset. The same night Mr. Wilmington talks to Stewart Wright and tells him what happened. He angrily tells Mr. Wright that he will in no way do any business with the firm if the young man continues to work there.

The next morning Mr. Wright asks Doug to come into his office. He starts by scolding him about what had happened during the party. Doug tries to defend himself by telling Mr. Wright what really happened.

"Sir, you've got to hear me out," pleads Doug. "I did nothing with that crazy woman last night. She was the one who made a pass at me! I would never do anything so stupid!" loudly exclaims Doug.

"Doug, please mind your tone!" replies Mr. Wright. "Look, you're an intelligent young man and therefore should never have gotten yourself into such an uncompromising position. I am sorry to tell you this Doug, but the firm has decided to let you go. We can't risk having negative publicity from a sex scandal involving one of our top associates. Also, I am warning you not to push this matter any further, including getting legal counsel. Mr. Wilmington is a very influential man, and you don't want to upset him any further!"

In truth Mr. Wright does not really care what actually happened that night. He is more concerned about losing the opportunity to do business with Mr. Wilmington's company.

Doug holds back the tears as he sits and listens to the final verdict handed down by Mr. Wright. *This can't be happening*, Doug thinks to himself. *This can't be happening!*

CHAPTER SEVEN
DOWN BUT NOT OUT!

Now unemployed, Doug is devastated. He starts to feel a deep sense of loss. He believes all the hard work and long hours he has put into his career will go down the drain. The same day Doug informs his family of what has happened. He is ashamed because he feels he has let them down. However, his family tells him not to worry and that everything will be all right. Later that night Doug calls up George and tells him of his predicament.

"Doug, I'm really sorry for what happened," says George. "Is there anything I could do?"

"No thanks, man. I just need some time alone to figure this out," explains Doug.

For the next few days, Doug spends time alone in his apartment. He mourns the life he has had until now, the life taken from him. He starts to drink heavily and sleep excessively. One morning as he is waking up after a night of excessive drinking, a vision comes to him. He hears Helen's voice repeating the key concepts she has taught him and George: "You are not a victim of the world... You have the power to choose what you want to see...You can change your experience for the better." Inspired by the vision, he forces himself out of bed. He is determined to get his life back on track.

Doug starts to look for work. He hopes to land a job with another large investment firm in town. However, his attempts fall short. He receives the cold shoulder from prospective employers. Word about the accusations against him has quickly spread. Since the financial investment field is a small-knit community, news spreads quickly from one company to another. Doug realizes his hopes of landing a job with another prominent investment firm are fading away.

A week later George calls Doug and asks him how he is doing. Doug tells George about his struggles with finding work. "I can't seem to find a company that will give me a chance," says Doug. "When they find out who I am, they act like I have some contagious disease. It's really frustrating," exclaims Doug. George tells him to take heart and reminds him this is a grand opportunity to apply the new ideas he has learned from Helen.

"You see, Doug," says George. "You can use this experience to become more in touch with your inner strength. Remember what Helen has taught us, 'You are not a victim of the world you see.'"

After another week of searching, Doug finally gets an interview from a smaller financial investment company. The hiring manager at this firm knows all too well the politics and dramas that occur at the larger investment companies. He tells Doug that they probably fired him because they wanted to maintain their image.

"Don't worry, I see your credentials and the experience you have, and I know you can be an asset to our firm." Doug is delighted this gentleman is willing to give him a new chance. He shakes the man's hand and tells him he won't let him down.

CHAPTER EIGHT

GIVE ME YOUR BEST SHOT!

As George lends support to his friend, he finds that his life is gradually changing. Not much so on the outside, but more importantly the way he is viewing life is changing. Day by day George gains more control over his thinking and how he perceives outside events. This change in thinking has given him more confidence in dealing with the pressures at work. He is less affected by rejections he receives from clients and the criticism he receives from his boss.

Additionally George's experience of always being a loner is slowly changing. He is drawn more to people and finds it pleasing to start conversations with strangers. He realizes that a simple change in thinking can lead to a more fulfilling life.

One day George meets with Pete Wilson before submitting a proposal to a large prospective client. The Kaufman Organization is a leader in the commercial real estate development industry, and landing an account with this giant could bring in considerably more business for George's company. As Mr. Wilson reviews

George's notes, he is agitated because he feels George has not pre-pared enough to make the presentation.

"George, I knew I shouldn't have given you such a big respon-sibility!" groans Mr. Wilson. "Look at your notes; you're missing important information about the company's sales and cost figures! You're going to make fool out of yourself!"

Although George has done extensive research on the company, Mr. Wilson is nitpicking and trying to make George feel bad. How-ever, this time George is determined not to let Mr. Wilson's behavior have any affect on him. George remembers he is not a victim here and can determine his experience as he wishes.

Mr. Wilson continues to degrade George on his preparation. "I can't believe you could be so irresponsible! Do you need me to hold your hand and take you to the presentation myself? Is that what you need, George? Someone to hold you hand?"

However, George remains calm and does not allow the criticism to affect him. He reminds himself that he is in control of his thoughts, not Mr. Wilson. Finally, when Mr. Wilson sees that George is not reacting to his criticism, he says, "Alright, go out there today and do your best. And don't let me down!"

As George walks out of the office he breathes a big sigh of relief. He can't believe he took Pete Wilson's best shot without getting upset. George is confident and ready to land the deal with The Kaufman Organization.

CHAPTER NINE
GEORGE'S CHALLENGE

One day as George is relaxing at home from a long day of work, he receives a phone call from his sister, who tells him that their mother has fallen sick and is in the hospital. After hearing the news, he rushes to the hospital to meet his father and sister. George enters the waiting room where his family is gathered. He immediately recognizes the worried look on his father's face. His father tells him that his mother has come down with some unusual form of cancer, and he breaks down crying. George quickly puts his arms around his father. As George finally comes to the realization of what has happened, he starts to feel a strong sense of emptiness in the pit of his stomach.

For the next couple of days, George is in great emotional pain. The only support he has known his whole life has fallen ill. George does not want his friend Doug to learn of his distress and avoids telling him of the bad news. He feels his friend has enough to contend with already. Instead he tracks down Helen Davies, the author. George is able to meet with her at her home. He tells her about the terrible events that both he and his friend have experienced and asks her why is this all happening now. Helen gently tells George she is sorry for all the things that have happened to him and his friend and that these experiences must be very hard to cope with.

Then she says, "George, I want you to focus and try to move past what you are feeling now. No matter how hard it may seem. You see, it is very tempting to lose sight of all the empowering ideas you have learned when something in your life challenges you and when you're hurting. But I say now is the time to use those same ideas that have brought you peace and clarity to help you move gracefully through these challenging experiences. You say, 'Why are these things happening now?' But I tell you that the events of the world, whether they are good or bad, will continue to happen. That is a given. That has happened all through recorded time. The only choice we have is how we want to see these events. Do we want to see them through the eyes of fear or love? These are our choices. In fact, these are our only choices. And I tell you that if you and your friend choose to use your spiritual eyes to move through these experiences, you will not only suffer less, but you will allow great healing to occur within your minds, and neither of you will ever be the same again." Helen pauses and then asks George, "Have you or your friend considered doing *A Course in Miracles?*"

George tells her he hasn't. "Well, if you want to accelerate your spiritual practice...I would like you to purchase the book now and get a copy for Doug as well. It will be the best investment you ever make. Not only do I recommend reading the text of the book, but also to start doing the daily lessons which are in the section titled 'Workbook for Students.' There are three hundred and sixty-five lessons that can be applied to situations you are faced with on a daily basis. The third section of the book, 'Manual for Teachers,' can be used as a reference for clarifying any questions you may have about the teachings."

George thanks Helen for the wisdom and advice that she has shared with him. He tells her he will make a commitment to start studying the *Course*.

The following day George meets Doug and tells him what has happened to his mother. He explains how lost he felt and that he needed to visit Helen to get some clarity on the situation. "The visit to Helen really helped me to get back on track and see the situation with my mother in a healthier way," says George. "I feel I have a choice how I want to perceive the situation. As I focus inward, I am guided to see a more loving perception of my mother. I have chosen to see her as what she really is, a perfect child of God who in truth is perfectly safe and cannot suffer anything. As I see her in this light, I feel safe and realize that she will be protected. Doug, I am very sorry for not telling you sooner, but I needed to meet Helen."

"No problem, bro, I can understand," says Doug.

"Hey listen, Doug, I got both of us a copy of *A Course in Miracles* that Helen was talking about at her workshop. Helen said it would help us with the problems we are facing." Next George asks Doug how he is doing.

"I'm doing well despite what I have gone through. It was tough getting fired from my last job and not being able to find any work. But you know I am learning to focus more on how I perceive the world instead of what actually is happening outside of me. This has helped me take more responsibility for my state of mind. Also I have more peace in my life and enjoy the simple things more," Doug explains, looking thoughtfully at George. "Most importantly I don't feel like a jerk anymore! I don't feel the need to be rude or arrogant with others. It doesn't get me anything by treating others badly."

George smiles as he looks at his friend. He can't believe how far both have come in taking back control of their lives.

CHAPTER TEN
COURSE TO THE RESCUE!

George continues to give support to his mother, who is receiving chemotherapy. The experience is still very challenging to George, and he is in anguish as he deals with the situation. But he makes a promise to himself that he will remain strong for the sake of his family. He feels a hopeful attitude will help his family to better cope with the situation. He is also determined to see this situation as an opportunity to bring more love and peace into his life.

As promised George starts to study the *Course* and applies the teachings to his daily life. His dedication to studying the *Course* is strong, and he brings it with him every time he visits his mother at the hospital. One day as his mother wakes from her sleep, she sees George sitting next to her reading his book. She asks him if it's a good book. He says it is and that it is helping him to see life in a new way. His mother tells him that she is proud of him for pursuing such a noble path. George feels very comforted hearing his mother praise him.

Next the two share many warm memories from the past. George's mother's eyes turn toward the ceiling and she says, "George do you remember the time when you were young and broke your father's favorite coffee mug? And you were so scared of what your father would do once he found out, that you locked yourself in your bedroom for the whole day."

"Yeah, I remember that," says George. "You know, the funny thing is that he never confronted me about the mug."

George's mother looks at George sheepishly, and says, "Well, the reason he never said anything is because I went out and purchased a duplicate mug. He never was able to tell the difference."

George breaks into a laugh and says, "Mom, you are the greatest!"

A few days later, as George is on the road visiting clients, he receives a phone call from his father urging him to come to the hospital immediately. George's heart sinks, for he knows the news can't be good. As he arrives at the hospital, he notices his mother's doctor talking to his family. The doctor spots George and asks him to meet with him in the hallway. The doctor tells him that his mother's cancer has spread, and there is not much he can do to control it. George calmly asks the doctor how long his mother will have.

"I'm sorry to tell you, son," the Doctor responds, "But we're looking at two to three weeks at the most." George tries to hold back the tears as he glances at his family, who are still in the lobby. George thanks the doctor and asks if his staff can do their very best to take care of his mother's needs. The doctor assures him that this will happen. Then George pauses for a moment before entering the room where his father and sister are. He makes a decision to remain calm for his family's sake. George walks into the lobby and immediately gives his father and sister a long embracing hug. He tells them not to worry and that they will get through this as a family.

The next morning George calls his work and is granted time off to be with his mother. For the next few weeks, he spends day and night with the woman who has loved him unconditionally. As time moves on, his mother's health deteriorates. She spends more time unconscious than awake. Although George is in deep pain, he remembers to apply the daily lessons from the *Course* to this situation. One of the lessons that he decides to stick with for a couple of days reads, "God is the strength in which I trust." The lesson is about giving your trust to God's strength and allowing him to be your safety in every circumstance. In practicing the lesson, George feels reassured and comforted. He starts to believe that a person can overcome any trial he or she faces by simply choosing to see it differently.

During the final days, George continues to muster up all the inner strength he has to cope with the situation. He finds that by remembering to practice the teachings of the *Course*, he suffers less and receives more guidance as he moves through the long days. George also serves as the strength to his father and sister.

One day as George is coming out of his mother's room, his father spots him and asks if he has a minute. "George, I want to thank you for all you are doing for our family," his father says. "I am very proud of you and the way you have handled this situation. So how about you come to work for me? I could use someone with your experience."

George gently looks at his father and says, "Dad, thanks for the offer, but I am really happy doing what I am doing." As George makes his way down the corridor, he feels very proud to finally hear his father compliment him. Internally George feels like he is finally succeeding in something. Although it is an intangible thing that cannot be measured, he feels his new spiritual practice has given him the opportunity to finally succeed in the world.

As the Harris family gathers to lay their mother's body to rest, the air fills with sadness, but a calm rest. Although the family misses terribly hearing the woman with the gentle voice and warm heart, they are relieved that the suffering is over for this brave soul. Once the ceremony is over, the family makes an internal pact to always remain close and love one another.

CHAPTER ELEVEN
ORGANIC FOOD?

Doug enjoys working for the small investment firm. Although the clients he is working with are not the big influential clientele he is used to, he enjoys helping everyday people make wise investment choices. As he applies the teachings of the *Course* on a daily basis, he is amazed how his life is being transformed from the inside out. Although his life is not as glamorous or exciting as it once was, Doug is experiencing more peace and happiness. He feels he has a purpose to life, and no matter what obstacles are thrown at him, he feels he can move through them in an empowering way. As Doug continues his spiritual journey, his outer life becomes a lot simpler. The once late-night partier and vacation-hopping executive has traded his old life for a more peaceful one. He finds himself attracted to activities such as meditation and spending time in nature. This one-time lady's man is not concerned about having relationships with women for the mere sake of filling a void. He is starting to feel he truly has everything he needs to be happy in life.

One day Doug goes to an organic groceries store where he sees a young woman who looks familiar. The woman is beautiful with long dark hair and hazel eyes. As they meet eye to eye, Doug asks the young lady if he knows her from somewhere. She tells him she knows him from the social functions she attends with her parents. She says her father is a partner with one of the investment firms in town. She then asks him whether he is Doug Peterson, the hotshot investment executive. She continues by saying, "You were involved with some scandal involving some businessman's wife, weren't you?" Doug is caught off guard by the woman's candor, but finally admits he is the one she is referring to. The young woman then asks, "So what are you doing on this side of town?" He tells her he's shopping for groceries. She tells him he is not the type she figures to buy organic food.

"Well, I recently changed my eating habits," explains Doug.

"Good for you," replies the young woman. She then tells Doug she has to run and that it was good seeing him. Doug tells her he did not catch her name. She tells him her name is Melanie Stafford as she hurries out of the market.

About a week later Doug again runs into Melanie inside the organic groceries store. He spots her in the fruits and vegetables section and walks up to her. They exchange pleasantries and have a lengthy talk about organic foods. At the end of the conversation, Doug asks Melanie if she would like to meet with him sometime to have a cup of tea or coffee. She says she would and tells him about a great mom and pop coffee house nearby. She gives Doug her phone number and bids him farewell.

A week later, Doug calls Melanie and sets up a morning coffee date. The two meet at the coffee house and enjoy a nice hot drink together. As their conversation turns deeper, Melanie asks Doug where he's currently working. Doug tells her about the difficulties he faced finding work after getting fired by the company he dedicated his life to, and how he finally managed to find work with a smaller investment firm in town. Melanie tells Doug that because of her father she has been around the financial investment community ever since she was a child. She attends the social functions to give support to her parents and to help with organizing. She says she understands the dramas that occur within these functions, but she tries to overlook them and focus on being a positive influence. Suddenly Melanie becomes quiet, and then she asks Doug if he would like to share what happened the night he was accused of doing something to that businessman's wife. Although Doug does not share the names of the people involved, he does tell how this woman made a pass at him and wanted him to spend some intimate time with her in her guest house, and when he refused how she made up a story alleging that he offered to sleep with her in exchange for business with her husband's company. Because his firm didn't want any bad press, they ended up firing him.

Melanie is appreciative of the fact that Doug shared this difficult experience with her. She also commends him for not giving up. Melanie then looks quietly at Doug and says, "You know, you are a lot different than I imagined you to be."

"How so?" Doug asks.

"Well," says Melanie. "I thought you were this shallow, womanizing, young executive who always got his way and would do anything to climb his way to the top."

Doug nods while looking thoughtfully at Melanie. "Until recently that was me. I had no respect for others or myself. I was short-tempered, sarcastic, and often times rude with others. You know, I didn't really care about anyone except myself. My primary goal in life was to make a quick buck and have a good time. But that's not who I am anymore."

"So what's the reason for the change?" Melanie asks, looking curiously at Doug.

"Well, I realized that my life was not making me happy, and that I needed to change my ways or else I would end up a lonely, miserable old man. Fortunately I was able to find another way, through an introduction to some powerful spiritual teachings. These teachings have shown me the place where I can find true peace and happiness. Although I have a long way to go, I know I am headed in the right direction."

"Wow, pretty deep stuff," replies Melanie.

As the two wind up their coffee date, both have gained a mutual admiration for each other. Doug tells Melanie he would love to meet her again, and Melanie assures Doug it will happen.

CHAPTER TWELVE
FACING YOUR DEMONS

A week later, Melanie calls up Doug and invites him to a family gathering at her house. Doug asks Melanie if it is a special occasion. "It's my parent's twenty-fifth anniversary and I would love you to be there."

The night of the gathering Doug arrives confidently at Melanie's parents home with a gift in hand. Melanie's mother greets him at the door. She welcomes him with a warm smile and introduces herself as Julianne Stafford. As Doug walks through the door, he immediately spots Melanie in the living room hosting other guests. He then hands the gift to Mrs. Stafford as he makes his way into the living room. He is a little surprised to see so many people at the gathering. The living room and dining room are filled with what seems are many relatives and friends. As Doug takes a little closer look at the different faces, he starts to recognize some of them. Then he immediately realizes that the faces belong to people he met at the various business parties while working for his former employer. He quickly infers that these people must be close friends of Melanie's father.

Suddenly Doug becomes very anxious and realizes he is getting himself into something he did not foresee. If these people recognize him, then he could be in for a very long and embarrassing night. Suddenly Melanie approaches Doug and gives him a big hug. "Doug, I'm glad you made it. I can't wait to introduce you to everyone." Melanie then directs Doug toward the various guests huddled in the living room. Doug starts to feel Melanie is leading him to the fire and wonders why in the world she invited him to a party where other prominent investment executives would be present. But Melanie innocently continues to introduce him to her family and friends as her friend Doug Peterson. Doug halfheartedly shakes hands with the guests and cringes every time he hears his name said out loud. After awhile he zones out the names of the people he is meeting and can focus only on his own name as Melanie says it aloud.

After awhile Doug pulls Melanie to the side and asks her if she knows that there are more than a handful of influential people from the investment circle attending the party. Melanie finally puts two and two together and realizes what she has done. She tells Doug, "Oh my God, I'm so sorry! I was so excited to introduce you to my parents and family that I totally forgot about what you went through. My father's friends are like family to me. And I never thought. I mean I did not—I am so sorry! You must hate me!"

Doug looks gently at Melanie and says, "If you weren't so cute, I would hate you. Anyway, I think you are a wonderful person and would never intentionally do something like this. So now where's the back door so I can sneak out?" Doug asks humorously.

"Nice try, mister," exclaims Melanie. "Although I may have not anticipated this happening, I still want you trust me and stay for the remainder of the party. And I meant what I said about introducing you to my family. Please don't worry about what my family will think of you. In the end I am only answerable to my parents, who have full faith in my making the right decisions. As for the rest who may not be thrilled by your presence, let them assume what they want. I want you to enjoy yourself and have a good time. Is that clear?"

Inspired by Melanie's talk, Doug replies, "Clear as a mirror." Although Doug seems positive about the situation, deep down he knows this will be a very challenging night for him; being around all these business executives will no doubt trigger many of the emotions he felt while being fired from his last job.

Before Doug joined the party, he centered himself and thought about what was important here. As he did, the daily lesson he was doing from the *Course* came to mind: "Love holds no grievances." The lesson is about how holding grievances shuts your mind off from its strength and allows you to forget who you are. Doug makes sure to keep the idea close to mind. For the rest of the party, Doug interacts with many people who, quite to his surprise, are genuinely interested in talking to him. He notices a few who intentionally keep their distance.

Later Doug meets Melanie's father, Gene Stafford. "It's a pleasure to finally meet you, son. Melanie's told me some great things about you," Mr. Stafford tells Doug.

"Well Sir, all the credit goes to you for raising such a wonderful daughter," Doug replies, shaking Mr. Stafford's hand.

"I hear you are also in the investment field," Mr. Stafford says, his face lighting up. "I must say you're a man after my own heart."

Doug, now feeling very comfortable, continues to enjoy his conversation with Mr. Stafford. Suddenly there is a commotion at the front door. It seems a surprised guest had come to join the party. Doug notices a distinguished gentleman enter the Stafford's home. Taking a closer look, Doug immediately recognizes him. The surprise guest is none other than Charles Wilmington of Wilmington Global Enterprises. Mr. Wilmington did not inform anyone that he would be attending the party because he wanted to surprise his old friend Gene Stafford. Recognizing Mr. Wilmington terrifies Doug at first, but then he catches himself and realizes that he can use this experience for healing. Doug continues to mingle with various guests and makes an effort to give each person his full attention; but deep down he knows that sometime tonight he will have to face his demons.

Later that night, while Doug is enjoying a drink with Melanie, he sees Mr. Stafford and Mr. Wilmington talking. Then he realizes the two men are approaching Melanie and him. Immediately Mr. Wilmington gives Melanie a big hug, and says, "Boy, haven't you turned out to be a beautiful young lady." Then he looks at Doug and asks, "And who is this handsome young man?"

Melanie proudly introduces her friend as Doug Peterson, not knowing the previous connection between the two. Hearing the name makes Mr. Wilmington a little suspicious. So he asks Doug, "So what do you do for a living, son?"

"I am a financial consultant," says Doug.

Mr. Wilmington looks at Doug and says, "So you don't say?" Suddenly Mr. Wilmington looks disturbed and says he needs to fill up his drink. Although Melanie and her father don't notice Mr. Wilmington's strange behavior, Doug is certain that Mr. Wilmington recognizes him. Next Melanie's father excuses himself as he makes his way back to the party. Melanie tells Doug she will be right back and needs to check if her mother needs any help.

As Doug is enjoying his drink alone, he sees Mr. Wilmington making his way back to him. Then Mr. Wilmington says to Doug in a sarcastic voice, "So you don't discriminate between older and younger woman, do you?"

Doug looks at Mr. Wilmington and says, "I'm sorry, sir, I don't get what you mean."

Mr. Wilmington responds, "Of course you know what I mean, and you don't look a bit sorry. You're that young hotshot executive who tried to solicit sex from my wife, aren't you? Is that what you do for a living? You try to take advantage of helpless women in order to further yourself in your career."

Doug butts in and says, "Sir, with all due respect, I did not ask your wife for anything or do anything inappropriate that night."

"Are you calling my wife a liar, you son of bitch?" loudly exclaims Mr. Wilmington, now completely in Doug's face. He pokes his finger into Doug's chest as he shouts insults.

Doug, however, remains calm and tries not to defend himself. He silently repeats the idea "Love holds no grievances" to himself. As other guests see Mr. Wilmington's aggressive behavior, they rush in to separate him from Doug before things get out of hand. Shortly after Melanie and her father rush in to see what has happened.

"Doug, what's going on?" asks Melanie. Doug quickly asks Melanie if he can see her privately. The two leave the scene, where Melanie's father is trying to calm down his friend. Melanie starts by asking, "Doug, why was Mr. Wilmington yelling at you?"

"You mean you don't know?"

"I have no idea!" replies Melanie.

"Well, it seems that your father is good friends with Charles Wilmington, from whose wife I was accused of soliciting sex."

Suddenly Melanie becomes light headed, faints, and falls to the floor. Fortunately Doug is quick to grab her and guide her to the ground. Some of the other guests see the two and rush in. Steven, one of Melanie's cousins, comes in to take care of Melanie. Steven, who is like a brother to Melanie, has seen the events of the party unfold. As he grabs Melanie from Doug, he tells Doug that he should leave the party; that he has done enough damage for the night. Doug is very concerned for Melanie's well-being but forces himself to get up and leave the Stafford's home.

A few days later, Doug is outdoors petting a neighborhood dog when he receives a phone call from Melanie. She tells Doug that she is sorry for all that occurred during the night of her parents' anniversary. She tells Doug that she has cleared up everything with her family and that he shouldn't worry about Mr. Wilmington.

"Although we all love Charles, we all know that when it comes to his wife, he lives in complete denial," explains Melanie. "Doug, I want to thank you for the way you carried yourself at the party," she continues. "You were a complete gentleman the whole night. I don't know exactly what you are doing with your life to make it more positive, but I have to say you are a joy to be around." Melanie then asks Doug if he would like to meet her for coffee someday. Doug tells her he knows a very nice mom and pop coffee house that a good friend once introduced him to.

EPILOGUE

A Course in Miracles can truly be life changing for people who come across its message. Students who embrace these teachings in their lives have experienced profound transformations. Happiness, a meaningful purpose, and a peace that the outside world cannot disturb are all experiences that dedicated *Course* students around the world have attained.

As you embark upon this new journey, you will find more and more resources made available to facilitate your understanding of the teachings of the *Course*. On the following pages you will find a reference guide that lists resources to help you on your path.

May the journey inward lead to your inner truth and peace. And may this journey allow you to transform the world around you.

RESOURCE GUIDE

A Course in Miracles
Foundation for Inner Peace
www.acim.org

Foundation for *A Course in Miracles*
www.facim.org

Foundation for the Awakening Mind
www.global-miracles.net

The Disappearance of the Universe: Straight Talk about Illusions, Past Lives, Religion, Sex, Politics, and the Miracles of Forgiveness
By Gary R. Renard
www.garyrenard.com

Accept This Gift: Selections from "A Course in Miracles"
Edited by Frances Vaughan, PhD, and Roger Walsh, MD, PhD

One Again: A True Story of the Power of a Different Kind of Forgiveness
By Linda Jean McNabb

The Journey Inward: Key to Everlasting Peace and Happiness

Forgiveness is the Home of Miracles: A Personal Journey through the Workbook of "A Course in Miracles"
By Robyn Busfield

Take Me to Truth: Undoing the Ego
By Nouk Sanchez & Tomas Vieira
www.takemetotruth.com

The Message of "A Course in Miracles": All Are Called, Few Choose to Listen
By Kenneth Wapnick, Ph.D

The Universe Is a Dream: The Secrets of Existence Revealed
By Alexander Marchand
www.alexandermarchand.com

A Course in Miracles: The Movie: Dr. Kenneth Wapnick, Gary Renard, iKE ALLEN, Nouk Sanchez, Tomas Vieira & others DVD

www.ingramcontent.com/pod-product-compliance
Lightning Source LLC
Chambersburg PA
CBHW071348130626
46556CB00005B/2079

* 9 7 8 0 6 1 5 4 7 5 5 2 3 *